THE LOST
PLANTATION
OF
BUFORD COLLEGE

MAX WINTERSON

Sonny's Big Cat Eyes
Publishing®

The Lost Plantation of Buford College.
First Edition

Sonny's Big Cat Eyes Publishing®

SonnysBigCatEyes.com

ISBN: 978-0-9985653-4-7

Printed in the United States of America.

For the Men in Butternut & Gray, I hope that their

sacrifice and legacy is never forgotten.

Chapter 1

Nashville, Tennessee 1864

"It is cold out here tonight! This standing guard on picket duty is not what I envisioned when I signed my name down for enlistment in the Confederate Army of Tennessee. A fella could freeze into a statue out here." Tim pulled off his backpack and blanket roll to prepare for much needed sleep after ending his guard duty.

John paused the whittling he was doing and then pulled his blanket tighter around his grey overcoat. "I heard that two of our boys died from the cold yesterday."

Tim sat down on his bed roll, warmed his hands next to the fire, and then laid his canteen, cartridge box, and haversack next to the tree behind him.

"Tim, for goodness sakes watch out! Your ammunition is rolling out of your cartridge box. Two of your Enfield cartridges rolled out on the ground next to the tree there. Don't none of us have any ammunition to spare like that. You'll be in trouble when the Yankees are moving in on ya and you ain't got any ammunition in your cartridge box," John said, as he pointed the tip of his knife at Tim.

"Oh! Thanks. What's that you're whittling on? Looks like brass," asked Tim.

"I've been picking up these Hardee hat pins since Atlanta. I've collected several variants of hat pins but these are my favorite. I am carving out the Yankee stuff on them and keeping the eagles to make rebel hat pins. I traded two of these eagles for a pair of shoes last week."

Tim looked down at his feet, "I hope that we get some shoes soon. These rags on my feet are the curtains a few of us pulled out of the Plater House up there. I can't believe we still don't have shoes. Marched all the way from Atlanta barefoot. How much more are they gonna expect from us?"

"Well at least we have some food tonight. That one ear of corn a day while marching across Alabama sure didn't cut it." John stirred the stew simmering over the campfire.

Francis, a soldier wearing Confederate States Navy buttons, scooted closer to the fire. "I agree with you. This is some tough duty. I thought we had to go without while in the Navy, but this is ridiculous by comparison. I never dreamed I would see soldiers, such as yourselves, who keep marching with no clothes, shoes, or food. Out on the big ocean, we did run into some disease, scurvy, and deprivations, but here with the Army of Tennessee, it is a way of life." Francis inhaled on his tobacco pipe causing the tobacco in the pipe bowl to glow bright orange. He looked off in the distance, then back at the frozen ground.

John furrowed his eyebrows, stared into the fire and then looked down, "Well, I'll take my chances on dry land. If I get tired of this soldering, I'll have somewhere I can run to. Out on the ocean you are trapped on that boat."

Francis, with pipe smoke now swirling about him, looked up. His piercing blue eyes met John's. "There are some benefits to being back on land. I do enjoy getting more letters from home." Francis raised an eyebrow and smiled. "I have been corresponding with a girl of the fairest persuasion in my home town. I have two more ladies that I will court, if that one doesn't work out." Francis looked over at the Plater House and continued to puff on his pipe.

John tasted the stew. "Well, aren't you the lucky one."

John and Tim both laughed.

"Laugh all you want, but mark my words, whatever happens, we are going to be heroes forever. I tell you that future generations will spend their leisure time looking for the one Navy button that popped off of my jacket last week when we were marching through Brentwood."

Tim whispered to John, "He sure ain't lacking in ego."

"Gentlemen, the story of the stand we have taken against tyranny will be frozen in time. You should have heard some of the speeches our Captain Raphael Semmes of the CSS Alabama gave us. The brave lads we lost on so many battlefields deserve to be immortalized."

"The boys in grey definitely deserve 'memorializing' for the hell they've gone through these last four years," John continued to stir the stew with a sorrowful look on his face.

Tim, shivering, said, "My ma and pa begged me not to enlist. If we survive for a little longer, we will have a fantastic story to tell when we're old men. I hope that we will be heroes and have all the girls to court that we want."

John started dipping the contents from the large cast iron pot into some smaller bowls. "Alright then 'heroes,' stew is ready."

Chapter 2

Glen Leven Mansion on the Franklin Pike in Nashville, Tennessee was a bustling place in December 1864. Hood's thirty thousand Confederates had advanced on Nashville and were set up for a showdown against General Thomas's Union troops that were entrenched in Nashville, Tennessee.

Confederate General Steven D. Lee had made his headquarters at the Glen Leven Mansion. A roaring fire was going in the front parlor room and soldiers were coming and going with dispatch orders for the thinly stretched Army of Tennessee. The Confederate line ran from, soon to be permanently named, Kelly's Point to Granbury's Lunette.

Bishop Quintard sitting in a plush red velvet chair looked across the room and outside at the cold snow encrusted landscape. He rubbed his chin and said to General Lee, "I am going over to give my regards to the Platers. Please send a dispatch to General Hood at Traveler's Rest to be expecting my arrival later this evening."

"Be careful out there, Todd. You slip and fall you could break your hip."

The Bishop rode in a carriage from the Thompson House over to the Plater House, maneuvering through the frozen landscape that had become almost too dangerous for horseback riding. Bishop Quintard had left his loyal old war horse just north of Franklin due to the slippery conditions. Many of the steeds were losing their footing in the wintery conditions, including the commanding General John Bell Hood's horse. His horse had slipped, below Spring Hill, tumbling the General hard onto the frozen ground. A powerful ice storm had now descended on Nashville giving an eerie, other worldly look to the gentle rolling hills.

As Bishop Quintard arrived at the Plater's home, General Edward Johnson rode up on his sure footed steed. General Johnson had returned from riding out to check on how the work on the Confederate redoubts was going.

"Hello, Bishop Quintard. Be careful getting out of that carriage. The ground is slippery. Don't want you to injure yourself." General Johnson proceeded to dismount, teeth gritted, he jerked his trademark club, also used as a walking cane, out of its saddle holster.

The bishop climbed out of the black carriage, drawn by two black horses. "Ed, you look a little agitated. You're not fixing to hit someone with that big stick, I hope."

"Well, Todd, I can think of a few folks who I'd sure like to whack with this stick. From Columbia to Spring Hill, we didn't stop marching till eleven o'clock. My men collapsed into sleep. I am sure you've heard the rumors but I am going to set the matter straight. I went out to the pike at one thirty and there were no Yankees. They were gone before we got there."

Bishop Quintard rubbed his head. "The Yankees must have snuck by the entire Army of Tennessee."

General Johnson with a confused look stopped and looked at the Bishop. "Todd, I am a little deaf, but I am confident that I or one of my men would have heard an army marching by us."

Bishop Quintard looked down at the frozen ground, being careful with his steps. "The evening's conditions, our timing, and the orders given were not in our favor."

General Johnson lost his wind, walking up towards the Plater House, he paused and leaned on his stick. "Not in our favor! That is a hell of an understatement. I knew when they sent us into Franklin at eight o'clock at night under a new moon that it was going to be an utter disaster. It was completely dark and I think a lot of our boys got hit by our own shooting. We couldn't see anything. I am disgusted with the waste of life at Franklin."

"I agree with you Ed. It was the most dreadful day I have ever seen."

The two grey clad Confederates paused on the west veranda. "Todd, I'm gonna say something that I don't want recorded in any official reports. The fight at Franklin was unnecessary. Six thousand men gone! Six of our best general's dead. A third of my boys gone! In my thirty years of experience, every time I have seen a night attack, it ends the same way... many men needlessly killed and wounded."

"You know Ed, you don't have to worry about me sharing your views. I can tell you that I have heard the same thing from many other men. You are not alone."

Chapter 3

West Veranda View

General Loring, upstairs studying battle plans and the strength of the fortifications with his staff officers heard Bishop Quintard's voice outside on the west veranda. "Please excuse me for a few minutes. I will be back shortly. Make sure all of the redoubts have sufficient ammunition."

General Loring entered the downstairs parlor of the magnificent two story, Italianate style country home with its wrap-around porch, built by the Platers in the 1850s.

General Edward Johnson followed Bishop Quintard inside using his signature club as a cane.

9

General Loring greeted the two veterans at the door of the Plater House, "Bishop Quintard, it is good to see you today my friend. General Johnson, are the fortifications going as planned, I hope everyone is ready out there?"

Bishop Quintard reached his hand out and shook hands with the general. "General Loring, I had to get over here to visit my patrons, the Platers. You're not overworking yourself, I hope."

"No, far from it. I don't intend to catch pneumonia from this insane weather we are trying to fight in. I cheated death before thanks to you. I might not be so lucky again. We should be in winter quarters right now. We lost three men from the freezing temperatures last night. We will improvise. I think we can give a good fight to the Yankees."

Mrs. Plater invited the generals and Bishop Quintard into the mansion's front sitting room for coffee. "It looks like General Thomas is finally going to be leaving Nashville for good. I am so happy to see the Army of Tennessee here in Nashville. Y'all are going to put an end to this ruthless invasion of our beloved Southland."

General Loring leaned forward, his elbow on his knee. He picked up his coffee, the cuff buttons on his grey Confederate officer's frock coat glittering, "That is our hope. If we can draw them out of their fortifications, we have our best chance of running them out of here. The Union entrenchments in Nashville are strong, but there is not a tougher group of men than what we have in our Army of Tennessee. We have a good line of strong redoubts that General Johnson has been out inspecting today."

"Hell, Bill, excuse me ma'am, we are stretched pretty thin. I would like to see some reinforcements sent to us! We'll make the best of what we have, but I am a little concerned about the troop numbers. Lost nearly half my boys at Franklin."

"We'll get there, Ed. Right now, we have got to strengthen our redoubts. We can't count on any reinforcements. Let's enjoy the coffee Mrs. Plater has prepared for us." General Loring looked over towards the Platers, "I will be glad once this war is over. We have lost so many brave men."

Mrs. Plater glanced down bit her lip and asked, "General Loring, do you have any plans for after the war?"

"Well ma'am, I've spent a great deal of my life traveling all over North America, fighting just about everyone. I would like to travel back overseas for some adventure. Specifically, Egypt and the Holy Land. I have taken an interest in Egyptology. I visited there before the war, and it is a remarkable place filled with ancient history."

General Loring pulled a medallion out of his pocket. "I found this in New Mexico amongst the belongings of an Apache warrior that was killed in battle," General Loring handed the medallion to Mr. Plater.

"This is an interesting relic, what do these symbols represent?"

General Loring pointed towards the medallion, "You see, this side is pretty easy. There are four stars around the side and then five smaller stars in the center. The Indians received peace medals from travelers and sutlers. When the Indians received these peace medals, they would make these symbols to represent the stars on the United States Flag."

"Yes sir, I can see the stars. How remarkable." Mr. Plater continued to examine the artifact.

"Many of these medallions came from Europe and originally would have had an image of the leader of a European country on its face. The Indians smoothed the face off and created these symbols. This one is a real mystery. The symbols on this side are Egyptian hieroglyphs which are far older than anything modern settlers have brought to North America. I have done a good bit of studying and research interpreting the symbols. I plan to return to Egypt to see if I am right about what the symbols represent."

Mr. Plater handed the medallion to Mrs. Plater, who examined it and then turned to General Loring. "What do you think you will find in Egypt?"

General Loring smiled. "I hope that the medallion leads me to a room full of gold and treasure. I'll enlist Ed and we'll leave no stone unturned in an expedition to find the treasure. And when we do, we'll split it. Ed has plans to marry soon. He can set up house with a beautiful belle on that farm of his."

Mrs. Plater handed the medallion back to Mr. Plater and got up to pour more coffee into everyone's cup.

General Loring leaned back in his chair, took a sip of coffee, then said, "I'll take my half and lead a few more expeditions, then settle down to write my memoirs. I'll be a soldier forever. That is my calling. It is the only life that I have ever known and the way I see it, the only life I plan on ever knowing."

Mrs. Plater smiled and looked over at General Loring, "How commendable, General Loring. But a beautiful lady might change your path."

General Loring cleared his throat. "I'm afraid that love and war haven't been a good mixture for me. I've written letters to a lady love of mine but have only visited her a few times." He leaned forward and looked straight into Mrs. Plater's eyes. "There's been no time for endeavors of romance. There's always been a fight that's called me away to service and duty."

Mrs. Plater looked away from General Loring's sharp gaze and reached for her coffee.

Bishop Quintard looked from Mrs. Plater to General Loring. "Bill, you must tell Mr. and Mrs. Plater your story of going out on the Oregon Trail. My friends, General Loring here could have made the devil himself fall in line on that expedition. Never before were so many rascals and misfits gathered together in one army."

General Edward Johnson lifted his shaking hands and took a sip of his coffee. General Johnson's eye fluttered at Mrs. Plater, somewhat aggravating Mr. Plater.

"General Johnson, do you have something in your eye?"

Ed looked down. "You must excuse an old soldier. My eye flutters due to a Mexican bullet to my head while in service to my country during that troublesome time."

Mr. Plater leaned back on the sofa. "My apologies, sir. You have surely seen more than your fair share of war."

Mr. and Mrs. Plater couldn't believe their good fortune to have so many famous people gathered together in their parlor.

General Loring leaned back in his chair and looked off with a distant gaze remembering his Oregon expedition. "Ah yes! That was the Gold Rush of 1849. We were sent to keep order, as the settlers made their way out west. Many of those settlers had no idea what they were getting into. Entire families were wiped out by cholera. I recruited that army from nothing. Men from Ireland and Germany. Had some good officers who stayed to themselves and did their duty. Any rascals were conditioned to military life real quick."

General Loring took back his medallion from Mr. Plater. "I picked up my first book on Egyptology during that expedition. We would trade with the civilians for books and things. That was a tough time. Many of the men died from heat stroke, not being accustomed to the climate of that region." General Loring placed his cherished medallion down on the coffee table and sat back in his chair, admiring the relic, and reminiscing.

General Edward Johnson raised his hand in an attempt to get a word in, "I've known General Loring for a long time. He is the toughest commander I've ever seen. We have fought in many campaigns together. They don't call Bill 'Old Blizzards' for nothing."

Mrs. Plater asked, "General Johnson what would you like to do after the war?"

"I have always thought that I might be a good farmer. I want to marry and enjoy nice, quiet days. You know, like sitting on a porch in the evenings, enjoying the sunset."

"That sounds lovely. Where do you hope to enjoy those days?"

"Preferably somewhere in an independent Confederate States of America."

Mrs. Plater smiled. "I imagine many soldiers share your dream to enjoy some quiet days."

"Yes ma'am. War is a rough business. You would not believe the way they treated the prisoners on Morris Island, South Carolina. The men that endured the heat and depravities in the hull of that prison boat last summer have forever earned the name 'The immortal 600.' There was one young captain named Thomas Perkins that kept on escaping from the Morris Island stockades only to be recaptured each time. Miserable place it was."

Mrs. Plater started to fan herself. "My goodness. Yes, the South has suffered long enough. I hope this war will soon be over."

Chapter 4

John and Tim were pulled off of their picket duty at the Plater House and joined the rest of their regiment with General Sears and General A.P. Stewart at redoubt number one near the front lines.

"Tim, that cough of yours is getting worse. You ought to see a doctor and see if you can get some medicine."

"I know John, but supplies are short. I checked and they said they didn't have any medicine to spare."

"Well, at least you have a warm coat now. That was nice of Forrest's Cavalry to give you that coat they confiscated from the Yankees at Johnsonville. Your old coat was in absolute tatters."

Tim coughed. "I bet ya that in a hundred years someone will shuffle through the dirt at this redoubt and pick those buttons up as souvenirs."

"You sound like that soldier from the Navy. Boasting about your old buttons, like any of this will matter in a hundred years." John stroked his beard.

An older soldier looked over after taking a puff on his pipe. "Y'all need some medicine? There's a doctor off of Granny White Pike that has tons of medicine bottles for just about everything. We stumbled on the doctor's place while bartering for food yesterday."

"I doubt that I can find it in the dark."

"Why sure you can. I'll draw you a map."

Tim took the map from the soldier and examined it, tracing the route with his finger, the camp fire glowing behind the paper.

The older soldier said, "Crazy that an order was given that no one was to have camp fires. We are fortunate to have good leaders here in our regiment that will ignore such insane orders. Some of our boys in other regiments are dying from the exposure to this weather."

Tim coughed again, a little harder. "I'm beginning to feel like one of those boys. This is a good map. I think I can find this place."

John wrapped his coat tighter around himself, "No one will know you're gone. Leave your bed roll here with your rifle and we'll cover for you. They'll think you're asleep."

"Alright, I am going to make a dash for it."

Tim located the house after a short walk down Granny White Pike. The doctor at the house heard a knock at the door and peeped out the window. He saw the young soldier and was leery when he saw that the soldier was wearing a blue coat. The doctor turned away from the window. He then heard the soldier start coughing. He looked out again and noticed the soldier was wearing a CSA belt plate. The doctor opened the door and waved Tim into his house looking both ways up and down the street to make sure no spies were watching.

"Young man, come on in to the parlor here. We'll get you fixed up. Tim came in and sat down in a chair at a table. A nice fire was going in the room's fireplace. "Here, I want to examine you. Oh my, you are burning up with fever."

"Sir, I heard that you might have something to fix my cough. I've got to get back to my regiment soon."

"You stay out there tonight and you most certainly will die. I'll send word to your captain that you are very ill. Don't worry, I've assisted other soldiers and no one has been marked for desertion yet. Now, I want you to drink this and rest in bed tonight."

Tim crawled under the covers and fell asleep in seconds. Deep in the night, a light awakened him. A bookshelf looked like it was partially swung out into the room and a well-dressed man in a vest and suit walked through the entrance with a lit candleholder. The entrance behind the bookshelf was lined with bricks. Tim felt a draft on his face and pulled the covers up to his eyes.

The next day Tim said to the doctor, "I thought I saw a man here in the room last night."

"Must've been the fever."

"No sir, I don't think so. What is going on here?"

The doctor cast a concerned look towards Tim. "Look, I need you to keep what you saw last night a secret. You must not mention it to anyone. The man you saw is a member of the Confederate Secret Service and he funnels information out of fortress Nashville. You are doing much better today. I have informed your captain of your health situation and that you need to stay here and recover. He is fine with it. Just rest, we should have you back to your company tomorrow."

Early the next day, cannon fire startled Tim awake. The doctor burst into the room that Tim was resting in, "You had better make a run for it! The entire Yankee army is on the move, and I don't think the Rebels can hold them back!"

"What do I owe you sir? I would have died without your help."

The doctor smiled. "Come back by here after the war to let me know you made it safely through the battle. Godspeed!"

Tim donned his Yankee coat and darted out of the house running as fast as his legs would carry him. The Union army was soon right upon him. Tim darted into the thickest bush he could find and burrowed himself under some leaves. He did not dare peek out of his hiding place as the enemy was all around him and he was afraid of being caught. At dusk, Tim moved out in the direction where the Union army had charged towards. He picked up a discarded rifle and U.S. cartridge box on the way.

Tim was stopped at the line between the Union and Confederate armies close to the Plater House.

"You don't want to go any further. The Rebels are right over there. We are the advance skirmish line."

Tim drifted over to the right of the Union soldier and in the darkness commenced to crawl towards the Confederate lines.

A Confederate soldier yelled out, "Halt or I'll shoot! Surrender Billy Yank!"

"John, is that you? It's Tim, don't shoot!"

"Tim? Oh my gosh, I almost put a bullet through you. We thought for sure you were captured by the Yanks."

John escorted Tim over to the front of the Plater House. "General Sears is dead. I saw them take his body away.

God awful scene. Men shot and dead everywhere. Looks like we are moving out towards somewhere."

A button popped off of John's uniform as he turned to hear information from a solider nearby. John took a step towards the soldier to hear what he was trying to say. As he did, the puff rim block "I" button from his uniform was pressed down deep into the ground from his footstep.

A Rebel soldier walking by said, "A new line south of here has been formed. We had better keep up or we'll be captured!"

Chapter 5

Nashville, Tennessese 1912

Most of the students at Buford College, an exclusive all women's institution of higher learning, were walking on the campus grounds enjoying the cool, dry October air. The leaves of the large Oaks at the college were beautiful vibrant shades of orange, yellow, and red.

"Come on, Elizabeth! Today is gorgeous! Perfect weather for a game of tennis! I am feeling really good about my game today."

Elizabeth tightened the laces on her shoes. "Margaret! I have beaten you every time we have played tennis this year. You've got to give it up."

"Not today! Today is going to be all mine."

Elizabeth straightened her long grey skirt, part of her daily uniform at Buford College. She confidently strode over to her side of the tennis court determined to hand Margaret yet another defeat.

At the edge of the court she tripped over a round metal object poking out of the dusty ground. "What is that?" She said, as she knelt down and brushed the dirt away from the object.

Aggravated, Margaret walked over, "Elizabeth, what are you doing?" Margaret stopped and put her hand up to her mouth, "Oh goodness, that is a cannon ball left over from the Great War! You better be careful. One of my uncles had a mule killed when his plow hit a live cannon ball. I saw the destroyed plow. He said that his guardian angel protected him from the explosion. That cannon ball can blow up half of Buford College if it explodes!"

"Margaret, stop with the drama. The cannon ball has been here for this long; it is probably harmless. Look, it is already loose. I want to dig it the rest of the way out."

Elizabeth got a butter knife out of a basket nearby and dug around the cannonball, wiggling it loose, and freeing it from its home of nearly half a century. "There we have it out. Looks harmless to me. I'll take it over to Mrs. Buford to see what she thinks about it. Better yet, we'll have one of the old soldiers tell us about it when they stop off the trolley train at Buford Station on their visit this week." She sat the cannon ball on a towel in her basket.

"All of this is delaying the inevitable, Elizabeth." Margaret walked over to her side of the court, "You are going to taste defeat today." She got her first ever win against Elizabeth that day.

Chapter 6

Buford College, Spring 1913

Abigail and Gertrude boarded the trolley at Buford Station in front of Buford College, located in the country side just south of Nashville, Tennessee. The Glendale trolley line connected Nashville with the countryside and the local zoo. It was a lifeline and provided some resemblance of freedom for the girls of Buford College.

Abby and Gert had become the best of friends over the past year and were inseparable. The two were very excited today as the chaperon assigned to the two girls for their outing was the one they had hoped for. Their chaperon was a favorite of all the students at Buford College. Lillian, a thirty year old married teacher at Buford College, sat a few seats back from the girls on the trolley, allowing the two freedom to talk and gossip among themselves.

Abigail ran her hands over her grey, drabby, standard uniform dress, "I am so glad that Mrs. Buford is going to allow us wear nice dresses for the dance next week."

Gert leaned over to Abby, making sure their chaperon couldn't hear, "These uniforms are so stiff. There is no way we can dance in them. Probably couldn't even attract the attention of a suitable bachelor to ask us to dance wearing these old things."

Gertrude, seventeen, and Abigail, nineteen, were thrilled to be off on a field trip away from the college campus for the day. Both girls, being from well off families, were accustomed to the finer things of life. The two found the exact dresses they wanted after shopping at a few stores in downtown Nashville. Then they convinced their chaperon, Lillian, that a stop by the Glendale Park Zoo would be good for all of them.

"Abby, I always love coming to this zoo. It is such a peaceful, joyous place. I hope this zoo is here forever."

Abigail waved her hand at the beautiful birds flying and roosting in the large bird cage exhibit. "Well I don't know of any reason it wouldn't always be here, Gert. This park has been here since the late 1800s. If women get the right to vote, I bet we can make certain this zoo will still be here in a hundred years. I read in the newspaper that a large parade was held in Washington, DC in support of women's right to vote. I wish that Theodore Roosevelt had won the Presidency. It looks like our new President Woodrow Wilson doesn't support women's suffrage."

Gert with a thoughtful look said, "You're right, Abby. We'll keep pressuring Mr. Wilson on women's rights till he gives in. Women should have a voice in choosing our leaders." Gertrude threw a wheat penny into the water at the sea lions exhibit. "These sea lions are so playful. That one seems to be smiling at me."

"Well, let's hope we can get some boys to smile at us at next week's dance."

Gertrude put away her coin purse. "We won't have any trouble with that issue. Our dresses are going to knock them off of their feet."

Abigail and Gertrude laughed and continued with stories on gossip and current events as they passed by the bear, monkey, and raccoon exhibits.

Abigail and Gertrude returned to Buford College. Getting off the trolley at Buford Station, Gertrude looked down and spotted a silver Barber half dollar laying on the ground, "Wow! Look Lillian, I've found a coin."

Lillian walked over, looked at the coin, and plucked it from Gertrude's outstretched hand. Gert's smile instantly went away.

Lillian held the coin up in her gloved hand, "We will find the rightful owner of this coin! I'll take it to lost and found for you. If no one claims the coin I am sure Mrs. Buford won't mind if you donate the coin to the general college fund."

Gertrude looked down at the ground and kicked the dirt, "Well, thanks Lillian."

Lillian walked on ahead of the girls.

On their walk up the long walkway in front of Buford College, Abigail said, "You should have been able to keep that coin! Finders keepers, losers weepers. That saying goes back to Roman times you know! The exact terminology is Res Derelicta which means, 'Something that has been abandoned and no longer has an owner.' See I have learned a few things here at Buford College."

Gertrude shrugged her shoulders, "I should have kept my mouth shut and put that coin in my hand bag. Live and learn, I guess."

The two girls arrived at the front of the old, two story Italianate style mansion with its romantic double wrap around porches.

Abigail walked over to the rose bushes in front of the old plantation house. "The roses they planted this year are gorgeous. Look at these colors."

Lillian walked back out on the front porch, "Hey girls, I've recorded you two as being back, don't forget to initial the log book."

"Yes ma'am," said Gertrude, "We enjoyed our outing with you today."

"Well, it has been my pleasure. You two young ladies are always exemplary students." Lillian turned and snappily walked back into the college.

Leaning over to smell the brilliant roses, a round disc partially sticking out of the ground caught Abigail's eye. She looked around to make sure no one was looking, then picked up the disc and brushed away the dirt. Abigail became mesmerized by symbols she saw on the disc.

Gertrude walked over, "What's that Abby?"

"I am not sure. I think it's a medallion of some sort. Let's get inside. I want you to keep this a secret!"

Gertrude brushed her long auburn hair out of her eyes. "You don't have to worry about me. I would have liked to have kept that half dollar. I suppose we could get in trouble though."

Abigail pushed Gertrude on into the building. "Won't be any trouble at all if no one finds out! Come on along now."

Chapter 7

East Veranda View

A few days later Gertrude asked Abigail at lunch. "Did you find out what that medallion was? Is it valuable?"

Abigail put a finger up to her lips, "Shush! Let's have a picnic and I will show it to you."

The two girls planned a picnic, close to the fence along the trolley tracks, at the very edge and in the back corner of the expansive east lawn.

The two girls spread out their picnic blanket. They had egg salad sandwiches, pickles, oranges, and apples in their basket. They proceeded to talk about current events, and gossip, going on in Nashville and around the world.

Abigail said, "I would like to travel overseas, maybe to the Middle East and Egypt."

Gertrude finished a bite of her egg salad sandwich, "Egypt! Why in the world so far away? Let's plan a trip to New York City this summer. I read that the world's tallest building was just completed there. The Woolworth building."

"Gert, that medallion I found is quite a discovery. I will show it to you if you promise to keep it quiet."

Gertrude smiled. "I can keep a secret. Remember last year when you snuck out to see that boy."

"Oh hush, Gert! I could get in so much trouble if any of the teachers find out about that." Abigail's hand went up to her mouth and her face blushed red. Abigail then lowered her hand and smiled at the memory of meeting the young man. "Here, keep the medallion down on the blanket while you look at it."

Gertrude's eyes grew wide, "Wow! What do all of these symbols mean? This looks very old!"

Abigail pointed over to a bench on the other side of the walkway. "Well, I talked to the elderly Civil War Veteran that sits over there when he visits here. He said that this is an Indian peace medal. The stars on this side represent the United States Flag. The other side is where it gets interesting. These symbols are Egyptian Hieroglyphs. Using books on Egyptology in the Buford College library, I have transcribed the symbols to my journal with a translation beside each of them that decipher the symbols' meanings. I think this medallion will lead me on an adventure. Maybe to lost treasure."

"Oh Abby, can I please come on the adventure with you? I promise to keep it a secret."

Abigail looked down, off in the distance, and then back to Gertrude. "Well, you're the first person I have told my plans to. My mother and father are paying for me to go on a grand tour of Europe and the Middle East for my twentieth birthday and graduation. My parents have agreed to my trip as long as I have a chaperon. My mother's sister who has never married has agreed to be my chaperon. My aunt has been everywhere, all over the world."

Gertrude put her hand to her chest, frowning, "Abby, I wish I was older, and we could go on an adventure together. What will I do around here without my best friend to talk to? I will die of boredom at Buford College once you are gone."

Chapter 8

Buford College

Two children whose mother was visiting their big sister at Buford College were playing at the base of the large Oak Tree nearby. One of the girls spied something between the roots of the massive old tree. Both of the girls started digging on the green piece of brass they saw barely sticking out of the ground. The two children successfully pried the object out from under the roots of the tree. They brushed the dirt off the rectangle, turning it over in their hands. Their eyes grew wide, then they ran towards Abigail and Gertrude.

Gertrude and Abigail asked the children what they were doing.

"Ma'am, we found this under that tree over there. Do you know what it is?"

Abigale gasped as the child handed her the green patinaed rectangle, "Oh heavens! This is a Civil War belt plate from the great Battle of Nashville fought here in December of 1864."

Gertrude asked, "What do the letters C.S.A. stand for?"

Abigail brushed more dirt off of the belt plate. "The Confederate Veteran who visits and sits on the bench over there, wears one of these. The C.S.A. belt plates were illegal for the veterans to wear right after the war. They hid these buckles to keep them from being confiscated by the Northern army. He said that the letters stand for Confederate States of America. You two should show Mrs. Buford your find! She will love it. She may even give you a reward for finding it."

The children ran up to the main building to show off their find.

A slight rain shower began to come down. Abigail looked up at the sky, "Oh no! Just when our picnic was starting to get good."

Abigail sat the basket off in the grass. Gertrude picked up a corner of the blanket and the medallion slid off the blanket and stuck sideways in the bluegrass. Abigail walked forward to help Gertrude fold the blanket. Unknowingly, her shoe pressed down on the medallion, its edge cutting through the moist spring soil, sending the relic deeper in the dirt.

"Gert! Have you seen my medallion?"

"You must have put it back in your handbag."

Abigail searched her beaded handbag. "Oh Heavens! I must have lost it," she said as she dropped to her knees and ran her hands through the bluegrass searching for the lost medallion.

Gertrude with tears in her eyes bent down on her knees to help with the search. "I am sorry for losing your medallion! I know how much it meant to you."

Abigail turned to Gertrude, "It's not your fault. You are my very best friend. Besides I have a transcription of the symbols written down. I can still go on my adventure and maybe I can get my family to let you come along also."

Gertrude wiped away her tears. "You are my best friend Abby. I will make it up to you someday, I promise."

Chapter 9

Fall, present day

"Blake, man, how's it going? Just checking in to see if you have been out doing any metal detecting?" Carter was on his lunch break from his day job as a lawyer in Birmingham, Alabama.

"Carter, it's good to hear from you. I've been relic hunting a little but not as much as I would like. I've had to fill in on some routes for my lawn care business. No complaints though. I am metal detecting more now than when I was on active duty overseas. I've been thinking… I know we enjoy finding Confederate relics on the Duck River line, but we should try to find a good spot here in Nashville for metal detecting."

"That shouldn't be any trouble. I would think that Nashville is full of great places to detect."

Blake pulled into his driveway, got out and petted his Harlequin Great Dane, Roscoe, "Not necessarily so. There are lots of dead areas where the soldiers were just not there. The soldiers liked to gather around old home sites. I am researching a plantation site called the Plater House. I have made some map measurements and from Granny White pike, I think the Plater House was on the edge of a large hill that runs all down Crestridge off of Caldwell Lane."

"Keep up the research." Carter said, "That is how the good stuff gets found."

Later that week, Blake stopped by the local county historical archives. A lady at the front counter led Blake over to a desk where a historian was sitting, reading an old yellowed document. Tom Gunner, pulled off the protective white gloves he was wearing and stood up to shake Blake's hand. He listened carefully to Blake's request for information, "I know that a women's college named Buford College was located in that area in the early 1900s. The Buford College buildings were torn down in the late 1940s and no trace remains of them today. There should be some good research material on the college in the downtown Nashville Library. If my memory serves me correct, you can find the Buford College yearbooks there. It's possible that the college may have been built over the top of the Plater House you are looking for."

Tom rubbed his chin thinking, then continued, "There is an older gentleman in that neighborhood who would remember the college, and he should be able to tell you exactly where it stood. I'll write down his address. His name is Jack Thompson. Jack's a good friend of mine. Tell him that Tom sent you over. If anyone remembers anything about a 'lost plantation' it will be Jack."

*

The following Saturday, Blake and Carter knocked on the door of Jack Thompson's house.

Jack opened the door and Blake took the lead. "Mr. Thompson, we are working on some research of a Civil War mansion called the Plater House that used to be standing here in this neighborhood. Here is my card. A historian over at the county archives named Tom said that you might know the location of the Plater House."

"Well, I do know a lot about the history of this area. I have lived in this neighborhood my entire life. Come on in and please call me Jack. I worked downtown as a lawyer during my professional career; now I enjoy reading books on the Civil War. I am glad to see that you two fellas are interested in the War of Northern Aggression. The story of the Great War is not taught in schools today from what I hear; a complete shame. A society will repeat its history, especially if they don't even know it."

Blake and Carter walked in and gazed at the many Civil War books on the shelves. Carter jumped as something moved on the couch.

"Oh! Don't mind my pet raccoon, he is harmless."

"Blake, that's a possum on the couch! I thought it was a pillow at first."

Blake spoke up, "Jack, isn't that a possum?"

Jack looked at the critter that was now snarling at Carter. "What time is it?"

Blake looked at his watch, "It's about 3:30."

"Ah!" Jack walked over to the back door and opened it. "There's my pet raccoon. Come on in, boy." He gave the raccoon a banana.

Blake and Carter watched in astonishment as the raccoon moved over to a corner of the room, away from them, to peel open the banana.

"He's a little shy. Well, come on into my research room. I may have something that can help. There was a women's college in this area around the early 1900s named Buford College that was located off of Caldwell and Crestridge; here I have a picture of it." Jack laid out a large book that had photos of old buildings in it. "This structure next to Buford College might be what you are looking for. This large two story structure with the double wrap around porch upstairs and downstairs looks like it is from the Victorian age. The style of this house is what they call Italianate and it was only built from the 1850s to the 1870s."

Carter asked, "Do you know where it stood?"

"Yes, I do."

Blake motioned his hand back and forth, "We like to look for old Civil War minè bullets, buttons, and any items that the soldiers carried. We use metal detectors and we are hoping to get permission to hunt for any Civil War relics that might still be around the old mansion. We are always respectful of the landowner's property and we never sell anything. We enjoy the history."

Jack looked down at the pictures and back up at Blake, "The area has changed a lot. There are no signs of Buford College or the Plater House left. The last buildings from the old college were demolished in the 1940s. If you fellas like, I can drive you by the site of Buford College."

Blake said, "That would be awesome! But we don't want to interrupt your day or take you away from anything."

"No! No interruption at all. I'm glad you stopped by. It gets quiet living in this big house by myself. Only company I get is from these critters. I'm very grateful to have y'all's company." Jack reached for his hat, coat, and keys.

"We can drive if you'd like Jack," said Carter

"Oh no; it'll be good to fire up my old car. I'll let you guys out and I'll be right behind you."

41

Blake and Carter looked at each other as a fierce rumble came out of a car behind the garage door. The garage door raised and Jack pulled out in a 1969 Pontiac GTO Judge.

Blake said, "Wow, that is a real classic! Unbelievable!"

"I thought y'all might like this. I purchased this car new when it first came out. I love this old car."

Jack drove them to a street close by. "Now, let's see, I have to take a certain route to remember where Buford College was exactly." Jack drove them halfway down a very scenic street, "There! You see the large magnolia tree in that back yard. That is where the main Buford College building built around the turn of the century stood. The older structure with the wrap around porches stood a little off to the left and that might have been the Plater House. History does say that Buford College was built on the grounds of a plantation where the Battle of Nashville was fought. Like I said earlier, I don't know for certain when the older structure was built, but I think it is definitely a candidate for your Plater House."

Carter, in the back seat leaned to the front, "We appreciate the information, Jack. If there is anything we can do to help you out please let us know sir."

"Well, you might send me some pictures of what you find while treasure hunting. I am interested in all things Civil War related."

Blake asked, "Which houses do you think we should try to get permission from, sir?"

"I would try all of the landowners in this area. This was a very large plantation with a lot of buildings, I am sure."

Chapter 10

Blake and Carter met up the following Saturday in Nashville, Tennessee. Their goal was to try and get permission from the landowners to metal detect for Civil War relics around the sites of what they hoped were the Plater House and Buford College locations.

Blake said, "So far, my research shows that two Confederate Generals; General William Loring and General Edward Johnson had their headquarters at the Plater House during the Battle of Nashville. A lot of Confederate troops would have set up camp around the Plater House. They would have only been there for two weeks, but hopefully they dropped something good that we can find."

Carter grabbed Blake's shovel and one of his bags to throw in his Jeep, "If we start finding Confederate bullets, that will be a good sign."

Blake continued, "Also, the first days fighting at the Battle of Nashville ended at the Plater House. It got dark and the Federal army could not see to advance any further. A.P. Stewart's Adjutant, Captain Gale, barely escaped capture at A.P. Stewart's Headquarters at the Johns House on Granny White Pike. He rode to the Plater House where he reported that he met up with A.P. Stewart on the front lawn of the Plater House."

"That is some great research! Thanks for bringing me along."

"No problem, man. We're a team." Blake climbed into Carter's Jeep, "Another event happened in front of the Plater House. A Confederate General named Claudius Sears had a solid shot cannon ball pass all the way through his horse and partially take his leg off as he was extracting his men from Redoubt Number One. He wrote in this diary that he looked down and saw his leg dangling from the saddle and hitting some corn stalks as he and his brigade made their way to the Plater House. Upon reaching the front lawn of the Plater House his men lifted him straight up and off of his horse Billy. At that point, Billy fell right over onto his side, dead from the solid shot cannon ball wound."

"That is an incredible story! If that had happened to me I would have curled up and died right there on the battlefield. That guy was tough!"

Blake fumbled through his papers getting his handouts ready for the potential permission to metal detect from one of the landowners, "And get this... General Sears was more worried about his horse Billy than his horrible leg wound.

He was hobbling on one leg in the snow crying 'Poor, poor Billy.' He loved that horse. He had ridden Billy from Vicksburg, to Chickamauga, to Atlanta, and then up to Nashville. He had his leg amputated later that day. He survived the war and spent his remaining years teaching mathematics at the University of Mississippi, Ole Miss."

"A lot of history happened here. Well, here we are at the first potential hunt site. Let's see if the landowner will let us metal detect."

The landowner let Blake and Carter know that a few other people had hunted at the site many years prior to them. "They left me with a few artifacts including these bullets they said were from Confederate Enfield rifles."

Blake picked up one of the bullets from the landowner's hand. "Those are dropped Rebel Enfield bullets all right! That means a Confederate soldier had to have been standing right here. We'll show you anything we find and share also."

"You boys help yourselves. I also own the two houses over there. I can get you in over at those houses to metal detect also."

"Thank you so much," said Carter.

Blake and Carter got their gear out and prepared to start in the front yard first.

Carter adjusted the ground balance on his metal detector. "This is exciting! Been hunted before, and relics were found. With these modern machines, we should be able to find something."

"I agree. Just remember to keep your discrimination at zero if possible. That'll help us recover any targets that might be hidden by iron nails from the Plater House and its outbuildings."

Blake and Carter each found a handful of Confederate bullets. In addition to the bullets Blake found an eagle coat button and Carter found a cuff eagle along with a nice flower button. Both relic hunters find the remains of Civil War backpacks, knapsack triangles, and J hooks.

Carter removed his headphones and walked over to Blake, "No belt plates today. I hope all of these yards haven't been hunted."

"Got to have patience, Carter. We are going to find some good relics."

*

The next weekend rolled around. Blake called Carter on Thursday. "Are you up for hunting this weekend?"

"Nah, can't make it. I've got too many things going on this weekend. You go ahead without me and I'll catch up next weekend."

Blake said, "Well okay. I'll see if Vickie wants to join me. She is flying out to Iraq on Monday to coordinate a tactical mission for a military contract job so this will be some good quality time for us."

Carter looked out of his office window at the clear blue Birmingham skyline, "You are lucky your gal goes detecting with you. Try to find something good Saturday and send me a picture of the relics!"

"We'll see how it goes. Vickie's tried metal detecting some but mostly she likes to video my detecting adventures."

Vickie and Blake got permission on Saturday. Vickie caught the entire hunt on video, "Here I am, out here in frozen Nashville, Tennessee. It is so cold. It is about 30 degrees. I can't dig, my fingers are frozen and my nose is red from the cold. Blake, are you finding anything?"

"Nope."

"Can you believe how cold it is out here?"

Blake adjusted his headphones, "I was afraid of this, the ground is frozen, almost as hard as concrete, maybe the bullets are here and they're too deep for us to hear them."

Vickie walked over to an unnatural looking line of raised ground in the yard, "Here we are in the frozen earthworks of Nashville, Tennessee and we are finding nothing. I am here because I love my boyfriend and I don't want him to think I don't want to participate in his hobby. Well I am signing off. Oh! Blake's digging a hole, let's see what he finds. What are you digging on there, Blake?"

"I don't know. It sounds really good… maybe a can."

All of a sudden, an item popped out of the ground. Blake instantly knew what it was even though it was upside down.

Vickie zoomed her phone video camera in closer on the item, "Oh look folks, it is a glorious aluminum beer can from the Civil War!"

"Nope, look again, that is the back of a U.S. belt plate."

"Huh?"

Blake picked up the belt plate and turned it up right, showing Vickie the U.S. marked plate.

"Oh, wow! That is incredible!"

Blake held the plate up to the camera, "It has all the hooks and still has the leather in the back."

The landowner couldn't believe the find. Blake split the treasure with the landowner by handing him a hundred dollars since the U.S. belt buckle was the only thing found.

United States enlisted man's Civil War belt buckle

The next weekend, with the weather being warmer and much nicer, both Carter and Blake hunted the site.

"I can't believe this Blake, I have four eagle coat buttons, three fifty eight caliber bullets, and two sixty nine caliber bullets, and you have an eagle coat button, plus a handful of bullets. Are you sure you found that belt plate here? There are still tons of signals to dig. I have a hard time believing that the only thing you found was the U.S. plate."

Blake replied, "Like I said, I was getting a lot of signals but couldn't dig them. The ground was like concrete. I didn't give up on the U.S. belt plate because it sounded so good."

Chapter 11

The following weekend, Blake and Carter got permission at a place a little closer to the Plater House site. Many sixty nine caliber bullets were dug. Carter dug several more eagle coat buttons and then got a really good signal.

"Belt plate!" Carter said to himself as he carefully dug. Spotting a little green and then the unmistakable edge of an eagle sword belt plate Carter carefully excavated the plate so as to not scratch it. "Blake! I have an eagle sword belt plate! This is something I have always wanted to dig. I can't believe it."

Blake said, "Super nice, let me see! Congratulations! You have worked hard to get that and you deserve it."

"Thanks, Blake. Have you found anything else?"

"Yes. I was coming over to show you these strange bullets I found. They are very large and I have never seen anything like them."

"Blake, oh my goodness! Those are .75 caliber Confederate tower bullets. One of those bullets is the equivalent of digging two U.S. belt plates."

"For real? Carter you better come over here and see if you can dig one."

Carter said, while walking, "You never see those and they are seldomly dug. They were fired from a Brown Bess musketoon style English rifle. The Confederate Cavalry liked to carry those rifles." Carter dug a hole close to where Blake found the first two rare bullets. Carter smiled as he pulled a massive lead bullet out of the ground. It was the elusive .75 caliber Confederate tower bullet.

.75 caliber tower bullet for an
English Brown Bess musketoon rifle

Carter and Blake hunted for a while longer and then called it a day. The landowner was amazed by how much they had found in his yard. The landowner said "Y'all dug it, so you get to keep it."

Blake said, "Please at least keep a few of these bullets."

The landowner refused, "I watched you digging. Y'all worked hard for those relics. I think I will get a machine and try some of that myself. If you dig it, you get to keep it."

"Can't believe our luck," said Blake.

Carter replied, "It's not luck, Blake. You worked hard on the research for those relics. Vickie is not going to believe how much those Confederate .75 caliber bullets are worth, but she knows that you would never sell anything."

Blake said, "We are blessed to be able to enjoy such a great hobby. We'll be counting our blessings at church tomorrow."

Chapter 12

By the time spring had arrived, many more bullets and buttons were found. Blake also found a U.S. cartridge box plate.

Blake poured water on a button he had just dug, wiped away the dirt, and then admired an eagle with a patriotic shield on its chest. He took a drink from his water container. "Dug another eagle button. Some of these buttons must have been worn by Confederates. We are racking up on Rebel bullets and buttons but I was hoping we would find some Confederate belt plates by now."

Carter paused his detecting. "You have to remember that the Confederates were only here for two weeks.... not much time to lose their equipment."

Holding the button between two fingers Blake placed it amongst cotton balls in a protective container and closed the lid. "That is true. I am going to head back over to the county archives this week to see if I can come up with some more sites for us to hunt. It has been fun hunting this 'lost plantation,' and we are definitely finding more here than we do on the Duck River line or down in Alabama. Most of the stuff we are finding is Federal. I just would like to try and find a better Confederate site."

Carter put his head phones back on, "This is as good as it gets! We have to be patient."

*

Later in the week, Blake walked into the archives. The historian walked over to him.

"Blake, I am glad you came back in. I remembered after you left that I have some aerial photographs from the 1930s of the area around Buford College and the Glendale Zoo."

Blake said, "That is super good news! We are having a difficult time trying to determine exactly where the old Buford College buildings sat due to all the out buildings close by. There are Civil War period nails everywhere over there."

"You are more than welcome to borrow them. Here I'll show you what I can make out with a magnifying glass. I think you will need to have these negatives blown up to see much detail. I was originally using these to try and find Confederate earthworks. Didn't work out too well. I was able to find the Confederate lines much easier from the ground. I had forgotten about them."

The historian handed Blake the aerial photographs. "Please be careful with these negatives and return them. These are from my personal collection and may be the only ones that still exist. Too many things get thrown out or destroyed to my liking in these archives."

Upon having the negatives blown up and scanned for computer use, Blake saw the distinctive 'U' shape of the turn of the century Buford College building. He was astonished when he also saw the distinct roof of the Victorian Italianate style house very close by on the Buford College Campus. "The Plater House," Blake whispered to himself.

1938 aerial photo - Caldwell and Glen Leven Drive

1938 aerial photo - Caldwell and Glen Leven Drive
with modern street overlays

Blake thought to himself that he was lucky that the Plater House was in the picture. Jack had said that he couldn't remember when the Victorian structure was torn down. Buford College closed in the 1920s. By the 1930s, sharecroppers had started tearing boards off the side of the older structure and burning the boards in barrels inside the larger structure in order to keep warm during the depression era winters.

Blake overlaid the scanned aerial photos onto a modern map saved on his laptop. He lined up the roads from the 1930s photo with the modern roads revealing the exact location and layout of what Blake was becoming more and more convinced was the lost Plater House.

Close up of 1938 aerial photo – Outer drive crosses Buford
College Buildings. Evans Road intersects with Outer.

Blake was surprised once his overlay was complete. The Plater House and its long front walkway was a little further away from where they had been finding a lot of great relics. The long front walkway stretched out to what was called Buford Station and on across to the old Glendale Park trolley tracks.

The next weekend, Blake and Carter reached out to the landowner of where the long walkway once was in front of the Plater House. Blake, within ten minutes of hunting found an eagle breast plate... his first one. The two also found a lot of .69 caliber bullets and eagle buttons.

Blake walked over to Carter with his hand closed. "Guess what I've got."

"I don't know. What is it?"

Blake held his palm out. A button with green patina and an "I" for Confederate Infantry was resting on the palm of his hand. "Finally, something Confederate. All of those Confederate Generals gathered right here in front of the Plater House at the end of the first days fighting at the Battle of Nashville just like they said in their diaries and memoirs."

The two relic hunters continued their search for Civil War artifacts.

Carter got a strange faint signal that most relic hunters would not have dug, except that he had heard the exact same signal before in his test garden when he buried a U.S. belt plate at ten inches on its side. He dug the faint signal and pulled an unusual looking relic out of the ground. "I've found something!"

Blake turned toward Carter and removed his headphones. He thought to himself, it was always something good whenever a relic hunter said I've found something.

Carter showed Blake the round brass disc he had just dug.

Blake held the relic examining it, "I have seen something like this before. I think it is an Indian peace medal. An Indian smoothed out this side and etched these stars into this medal to resemble the United States Flag. But look at these small initials W.W.L etched here next to the stars. That has to be General William W. Loring who stayed at the Plater House during the Battle of Nashville. That is too cool. You have found a relic that was carried by General Loring."

Blake handed the relic back to Carter who turned the relic over, and said. "This is an awesome find! What about the other side? Are those Egyptian hieroglyphics that are etched onto the medal?"

"That is crazy Carter. Egyptian writing would make that medal way older than the peace medals I have seen online."

A few more relics were found by Carter and Blake, then they call it a day.

Arriving at their homes later that evening the two searched the web but couldn't find anything like the medal Carter had found. The mysterious medallion continued to keep its secrets as the days passed by.

Carter decided to reach out to his friend Rachel to see if she would examine the Indian peace medal.

He dialed her number, and she picked up on the second ring.

"Hello, this is Rachel."

"Rachel, it's Carter, are you busy?"

Rachel did not know what to say and paused while she thought to herself, my new boyfriend is not going to like an old boyfriend calling me!

"Hey Carter, what's up?"

"I hate to bug you, but we have found a crazy relic that we are stumped on. If I email it over can you pleaseeee take a look at it."

"Carter, I can help out with this a little, but I've got to let you know that I'm seeing someone and he's a little bit of the jealous type."

Carter said, "Oh, so sorry. Please just examine the item a little. There is no one else who can provide your expertise."

Rachel replied, "That is true, I am the very best at solving a mystery. Send it on over. Don't worry about what I said. It has been a long week and solving a puzzle is probably just what I need."

The next evening, Rachel poured herself a glass of her favorite pinot noir and opened her email. "Well, let's see what they've found this time," Rachel said out loud to herself.

In the attachment was a picture of the Indian peace medal with a description of the relic along with who they thought was carrying the medallion when it was lost. Rachel noticed faint images of more hieroglyphics that were barely discernable on the side where the stars were. The Indian who etched the stars had smoothed out that side so much that the images were almost completely obliterated. She put the medal through different shadings on her computer to sharpen the images. Rachel thought to herself that one of the faint images might be the side profile of an Egyptian Pharaoh. Most of the hieroglyphics on the smoothed out star side were too faint to make out.

Rachel spent a week studying and translating the mysterious Egyptian hieroglyphs on the medallion. Rachel called Carter the next Friday before her date with her new boyfriend. She got his answering machine. "Carter, you have definitely stumbled onto another treasure story. I've emailed you clues to a site in Egypt. *Bonne Chance* on your adventure. Call me tomorrow. I've found some other information. Bye."

Carter got home from a night of playing billiards at a local pool hall and saw the light blinking on his answering machine. He pressed the playback button and heard Rachel's voice. After listening to her message, he opened his laptop to pull up the email she had sent. Sure enough, Rachel had pinpointed coordinates to a potential treasure site in a Middle Eastern desert.

The next day Carter called Rachel, "Hey Rachel, I got your message. Sorry I missed your call."

"Carter, that medallion is old and I think it did originate from Egypt. The smoothed out side also has faint hieroglyphs on it. I've translated all of that and sent it to you in a second email today. In my research I also found an interesting diary online that was kept by one of the girls that attended Buford College. Her name was Elizabeth Shackles."

"Oh, Wow! Great job what does the diary entry say?"

"Hold on Carter. I've got that here somewhere." Rachel flipped through the research material. "Here is an entry in Elizabeth's diary; 'Gertrude once again proves to be someone you never tell a secret to. She told me that she would tell me something but I could never repeat it to anyone. Gert said that she and Abigail are going on a Grand Tour of Europe and that they will find a treasure in Egypt worth a fortune.'"

"Like Ben Franklin used to say 'three people can keep a secret if two of them are dead.'"

"There are more entries about Gertrude, Carter. After her and Abigail's trip to Europe Gertrude had a handsome man from Spain visit her at Buford College. Elizabeth said that the man introduced himself as a matador. The last entry about Gertrude reads 'biggest scandal in Buford College history. Gertrude has eloped to Europe with her matador lover.'"

"That must have been kept quite because Buford College prided itself on never having an elopement."

"Get this Carter, I found at the library the name of a girl by the name of Gertrude Fannin that attended Buford

College. There is no listing of her death. I also found on micro film an article where authorities in Spain determined that she eloped with her lover, a man named Sommes Delroy. My research shows that he was a matador in Spain at the time. The scandal gets worse due to the fact that he was married."

"Woah! That is some high drama. It sounds to me like they might have found the treasure and lived happily ever after."

"I don't get that feeling Carter. Gertrude didn't sound like the type to disappear. She had close friends and family. Gertrude and the matador vanish off the face of the earth at that point and time. There are no records of their deaths later. Nothing."

"Hmmm... that does sound suspicious, but who knows, love does make people behave strangely." Carter paused and sighed. "It sounds like a real mystery, Rachel."

"I've sent you an email with all of my research. You should take Blake with you if you decide to pursue an expedition to investigate."

"Of course. It'll be right up Blake's alley. You sure you don't won't to make another treasure hunting expedition."

"No way! I want to stay put in the good ole U.S.A.."

Carter hung up the phone after saying goodbye to Rachel. He opened his laptop and clicked on the second email. Studying the material, he saw where Rachel wrote out beside one of the faint hieroglyphics; Pharaoh? He rubbed his chin, astonished by the amount of research Rachel had done.

Carter called Blake the next day. "Blake, Rachel has deciphered enough of the clues on that Indian peace medallion to get us started on a new treasure hunting adventure. You won't believe this, but we are headed to Egypt to find to find the Pharaoh's Relic!"

www.ingramcontent.com/pod-product-compliance
Lightning Source LLC
Chambersburg PA
CBHW021026120726
47905CB00009B/3207